T

CHEETAH CUB

RUNNING CLUB

The Great Fox Chase

A Rapid Rory and Speedy Stella Adventure

By Philip Laslett

The Cheetah Cub Running Club: The Great Fox Chase

Copyright © 2021 to Philip Laslett

https://cheetahcubrunning.club

This is a work of fiction. Although actual places are used in some cases, all characters and happenings are fabricated.

Published by Runner Who Writes LTD

https://Runnerwhowrites.com

Editing and formatting by Let's Get Booked

www.letsgetbooked.com

Cover illustration by

https://agnessaccani.com/

Print ISBN: 978-1-8384944-3-8

eBook: ISBN: 978-1-8384944-2-1

To Rosie and Alice

Get your FREE copy of The Cheetah Cub Running Club PREQUEL: Where It All Began

It is 1921 and a cheetah coalition is struggling. Lack of food and water, threats from Hyenas at every corner. Reliant on Chaka, a young adolescent cheetah, to provide for them. The odds are against them.

How are they going to survive? What can they do to ensure their future?

Chad, a senior cheetah, has an idea...

Scan to get your FREE book:

LONDON IS RACING

The hairs on Rory's arm stood to attention, and he shivered. Jogging on the spot and shaking his arms in nervous anticipation, he focused, bracing himself for the words he had heard a hundred times before.

Suddenly, silence descended. The calm before the storm.

"On your marks, get set, go!" Rory rocketed forward, jostling for position among the other boys, girls, men and women who all had a similar intent. The silence had been abruptly displaced by the drum of people pounding the path of his local park at pace as they passionately strived for a personal best on the weekly Parkrun.

It was Rory's first opportunity to run with others since returning from Africa, where he had become a member of The

Cheetah Cub Running Club a few weeks earlier, and he was loving it!

Rory's start line anxiety was a distant memory, evaporating as he rounded the first corner of the bridleway in Dulwich Park, a short distance from where he lived in South London, England. The cool breeze was welcomed, and for a moment, Rory's mind transported him back to the African savannah over five thousand miles away.

He visualised himself running around the dusty club track with cheetahs, elephants, rhinos and warthogs trailing in the distance as he powered forward. Oh, how he missed Chiku, his favourite cheetah cub, and the rest of the gang.

"See you later, Rapid!" A voice jolted him back to the present. It was Stella, from his class. The girl laughed as she overtook him on the back straight. Stella was known as 'Speedy Stella' in school, for obvious reasons.

Rory refocused and set about catching up to her. Dodging between the other runners, he moved up through the field. By the third and final lap, he was right behind his adversary.

Stella could sense his presence, and whilst neither could talk as they breathed heavily; mutual respect was evident as they pushed on towards the finish line.

With a hundred metres to go, the two ten-year-olds turned up the throttle. Both sprinted savagely, searching for something special to secure success over the other. At fifty metres to go, Stella moved ahead. *Thirty metres*, Rory clawed back to be level; *ten metres*, *five metres*, both leaned towards the line, just as another uninvited body flowed past and crossed the finish line before the two bewildered, breathless battlers.

Who had taken them both by surprise? How could they be so blinkered on their own race and miss the foreboding threat of Fast Florence!?

"Why hello Speedy and Rapid, fancy meeting you here," Florence said with a wry smile. Florence went to the rival school in the area and loved beating these two whenever she could.

The group were joined by another regular at the run, Steady Eddie. "What took you so long?" he said with a big grin. Stella and Rory looked at each other, then back at Eddie. They were so consumed with each other, Eddie had steadily made his way with the lead group to finish ahead of them.

"Er... hi Florence and Eddie, well done. See you next week," Rory and Stella said in unison as they sheepishly walked towards their bags and put on their tracksuit tops.

Rory took a deep breath while Stella gathered her thoughts.

"Well, I've got to get back home for lunch. See you at school on Monday?" Stella asked.

"Sure," Rory replied.

"Remember, we have a cool trip to look forward to," Stella said, turning to leave.

Rory racked his brain, thinking back to Friday in class when his teacher Tom gave the details of the trip. Before he could ask Stella, she was long gone, and just a cloud of dust remained.

TIME TO BE A HERO

"Ah, yes, awesome," Rory said out loud to no one in particular.

He had remembered his class would be going to see the famous Roger Bannister Running Track in Oxford where sixty-seven years ago Sir Roger Bannister became the first person in the world to run a mile under four minutes.

As Stella had left, Rory surveyed his surroundings. He'd been to the park many times; now his second favourite place on earth, after The Cheetah Cub Running Club track back in Africa. The park had a lot going for it. The sports facilities, the playground, the café where he would feast on a snack and plenty of thirst-quenching water on a summer's day. The wooded areas, intriguing trees, and plants. Particularly the trees, which were ideal for climbing and hiding. And of course, the bridleway, which circled everything else and, married to the path which ran adjacent, magically turned into his weekend running track.

Rory came to a halt at a familiar oak tree. Leaning up against the bark, it felt like an old, trusty friend. Scrambling up to a higher vantage point, his mind raced back to the last time he'd been sat in a tree just before he found the cheetah cubs.

Gazing out into the distance, Rory sighed. The Cheetah Cub Running Club had not been in touch. I mean, how could they? They were thousands of miles away without the benefit of Wi-Fi in their cave (to the best of his knowledge).

Rory missed the adventure. He missed running in the African plains with his buddies.

But this was no time to waste. He had limited opportunity to get out of the house since his parents were keeping a much closer eye on him after his unauthorised jaunt on safari.

Something caught Rory's eye. It was another regular visitor to the park, Snuggles, a poodle with a touch of class about him. Rory enjoyed playing and racing with him.

"Snuggles!" Rory called after the well-kept dog, who unexpectedly ignored Rory and sped off towards the woods. He let out a big sigh, shrugging his shoulders. He jumped down from the tree to continue on his way, daydreaming about winning the London Marathon one day.

Rory had no idea how long he had been jogging in his dreamworld when a situation developing near the café brought him back to the present. He ventured over.

"My pride and joy, my wonderful Snuggles. He's gone missing," a hysteric lady wailed.

"Hello, Ms…?" Rory enquired.

"My name is Mrs Partridge and Snuggles, my beautiful black and white poodle has gone!"

This was not an uncommon conversation at the café at the heart of the park. Many a giddy coffee drinker had proclaimed to lose a pet, only to find them idly enjoying themselves in the adjacent pond or peeing up against one of Rory's oak buddies, much to the green keeper's disgust.

"Don't worry, I'll find him for you," Rory declared, shoulders back, puffing out his chest like one of his favourite superheroes. Rory loved taking on the role of local school-boy hero. He felt a newfound responsibility to help others ever since becoming a member of The Cheetah Cub Running Club, and it gave him an excuse to stay out much longer. Now was a good time to live up to his role, and he was confident his speed would allow him to catch up with Snuggles in no time at all.

"Oh, thank you, young man," Mrs Partridge said, sincerely.

"No problem. Do you have a picture of him with you?"

Mrs Partridge handed Rory a photo of her and Snuggles in happier times.

"Thank you, I'll be back with Snuggles as soon as I can."

Detective Rapid Rory was on the case!

DETECTIVE WORK

Rory walked off purposefully until he had rounded the corner, at which point, he moved into a full-on sprint.

He arrived at a small, wooded area, half expecting to find Snuggles, sniffing about or doing his business under a tree.

He wasn't there. *Hmm, maybe he's at the pond?* Rory pondered. It was late summer, yet there was a chill in the air. Not exactly the right temperature to take a dip.

He jogged over to the pongy pond. *Nope, no sign of Snuggles here either...* Confusion was written on Rory's face, his shoulders slumped. This would not be over as quickly as he originally thought." Rory straightened up and headed straight for the woods.

"Snuggles, Snuggles, I've got a bone for you," Rory fibbed. He would try anything to tempt the lost dog from his hiding place.

Rory continued deeper, further than he typically ventured. Pushing branches out the way, brushing past bushes, his mind wandered. *Had Snuggles been abducted by aliens? Had a gang of dog robbers caught him and sold him to a rich family for a bag of 24-carat diamonds? Maybe he had run off with Sniffles, the snotty-nosed spaniel who regularly poked his nose where it wasn't wanted?*

Whatever the reason for his disappearance, Rory was more determined than ever to find Snuggles.

He was now at the heart of the wood and was pleasantly surprised to find areas of the park he hadn't discovered previously.

Disillusioned at the lack of success in tracking down the lost pup, he sat down. If only The Cheetah Cub Running Club were here to help him.

After a few moments of self-reflection, Rory's gaze settled on a particular patch of greenery. Somehow, it didn't quite fit in. It was as if someone had coloured a picture and changed from using a crayon to a felt tip pen. Rory approached to see if his eyes deceived him.

On closer inspection, the branches were from palm trees amidst a wood of conifers. Had they been placed there to cover something up? Tentatively, Rory pulled the branches away.

He peered in closer to see a large tunnel.

Rory had upgraded to recording his adventures on a small Dictaphone he got for his birthday. "HQ, new suspicious opening found. Possible badger set. Er... correction, possible massive mutant badger. Over."

The tunnel was big enough for a ten-year-old to walk down while crouching.

Could Snuggles be hiding inside?

Rory's curiosity once again drew him into investigating further.

"I'll just go a few metres in. I've got my torch. It'll be fine," he reassured himself.

Light beam on, with a deep inhale of breath, Rory stepped forward.

FRIENDLY FACES

"Here we go again," Rory murmured to himself as he trudged down the tunnel, crouching on his haunches as the tunnel narrowed.

This was beginning to feel like a bad idea as Rory squeezed through another tight spot, banging his head in the process. He would be unable to turn back now even if he wanted to.

"Hey, Snuggles, are you down here?"

The tunnel surprisingly started to widen. Rory gradually lengthened his back as he focused on something very familiar. A door. Not just any door but an identical door to the door from the cave in Africa.

Rory tentatively knocked, took a step back and cowered. This time the door immediately swung open, and Raziya beamed back at him with a gappy rhinoceros grin!

"Finally, Rory! You made it! What took you so long?" Raz said, smiling.

Rory, mouth open as wide as the Channel Tunnel, was speechless.

"Come with me; we've been expecting you."

Turning the corner, Rory could not believe his eyes. He was right back in his favourite place, the same animal city he had experienced for the first time in Africa. How on earth had this happened?

A familiar voice caught Rory's attention. "Well, hello, fancy meeting you here!" It was Chidinma, the HQ cheetah leader, who revelled in Rory's confusion.

"I am sure you have many questions, Rory. We'll address them shortly. Let's go to the club first. The team will be delighted to see you."

Chidinma was of course referring to The Cheetah Cub Running Club. Rory had not returned to the humble racetrack since becoming their latest honorary member.

"Rory!" Chewe spotted him first and bounded over. The cheetah cub launched playfully at Rory, sending him backwards. Soon he was engulfed by the entire gang, giggling with glee. Elon clung tightly to him with his trunk. Joy and laughter filled the air. Chiku was the last to approach.

"Howdy, partner. I hear you are missing a dog," Chiku said, placing her paw on Rory's shoulder.

"Er… yes, I am, but how did you know that, and how on earth did you transport me back here so quickly? And why is there a door that looks remarkably similar to the one in the secret cave in Botswana now located down a tunnel in my local park in London...?" Rory asked with an inquisitive look on his face. His voice gradually increased in volume with each question as the enormity of the situation dawned on him.

There was a moment's pause.

"We'll explain all in good time," Chidinma replied.

"Great to see you, by the way," Rory said with a wry smile.

The group broke into laughter and conversation. It was like they had never been apart.

"Sorry to break up the reunion vibe, guys. Rory, it's time to talk," Chiku said.

Rory, Chidinma and Chiku sat on the side of the track.

"The primary purpose of The Cheetah Cub Running Club is to help animals and humans in need. We are a rescue crew first, runners second. One of our core values is helpfulness," Chidinma explained, handing over a booklet to Rory entitled 'CHEETAH CUB RUNNING CLUB: NEW MEMBER HANDBOOK.'

She continued, "When a new member joins the club, we open a portal near their home location so we can reach them quickly if they need our help."

Rory held up his hand.

"Yes, Rory?"

"What's a portal?"

"It's a tunnel or gateway between two faraway places that allows for instant travel from one to the other. We don't reveal this to new members right away to avoid unnecessary trips and attention on the club.

We also have portals that open near any running or racetrack around the world. We find an empty track after dusk, and the running club can use it to get our exercise in to stay fit and healthy whilst close to the action."

"Ah, exercise! Another of the cheetah cub values." Rory said, pointing at the list in the handbook.

"Yes, exactly. Now, we heard your cry for help in your search for Snuggles. It was only a matter of time before we found each other," Chidinma said with a grin.

"So, you've been here all along? In the tunnel, sorry portal, back to Club HQ?" Rory asked.

"Yes, from the moment you landed back in London," Chiku said.

Rory raised his eyebrows. Before he could speak, Chidinma interrupted. "I think it's time to help find that lost dog!"

MISSION CONTROL

Chidinma ran purposefully into the clubhouse. Chiku gestured for Rory to follow.

On entering the clubhouse, Rory walked down the entrance hall past photo after photo of happy reunited animals and people. Newspaper clippings and headlines dating back a hundred years such as 'Cardiff dog owner delighted as Rover mysteriously found in the Himalayas', 'Chimpanzee finds his way back to New York Zoo from Guatemala.'

"We've been at this game for generations," Chiku said after noticing Rory's intrigue.

"The running club was set up in the 1900s by a small group of cheetahs who wanted to encourage their cubs to channel their enthusiasm for running into a friendship group with other animals. Throughout the years, we started to travel more to experience running in different habitats. We uncovered other like-minded animals who loved running and wished to join the club, so we set up regional Cheetah Cub Running Clubs with a common set of values. As we became a core part of each community, animals in need would come to us for help, usually for assistance with manual tasks, such as fixing a bridge, or helping find food or shelter. Then we started to see an upward trend in rescue mission requests, due to being the fittest and strongest team available to help with the search. It became apparent this was a sweet spot for us, so we started to spread the word that we were available and willing to help. We were able to expand internationally after a chimp, who had recently worked at NASA and had been to space, taught us how to set up a portal to another country. This is a closely guarded secret to this day."

The pair walked past rooms full of maps and drawings, connecting the last known whereabouts of hundreds of missing animals. It reminded Rory of a police detective series his parents watched.

"More recently, we have diversified into helping humans. However, it comes with its risks. Obviously, they are not used to animals talking, or running for that matter, let alone solving their crisis. That's why we interact only with kids as our latest partners, then as they grow up, our network grows stronger."

Chiku paused and opened a door. "After you," she said, gesturing at Rory.

On entering, Rory stared at the far wall, which was covered top to bottom with artefacts. A map of the park stood out prominently as well as pictures of Rory, Snuggles and Mrs Partridge. The point of Snuggles' last sighting was marked with a timestamp:

LAST KNOWN LOCATION: COFFEE SHOP, DULWICH PARK, LONDON, UK.

DATE: 4th SEPTEMBER 2021

TIME: 10:30AM GMT

Rory laughed. "You guys have been busy."

Just then, Ranger Adia walked into the room. "Rory! So good to see you," she said.

Rory beamed at her. "You too, Adia." Adia had become a good friend to him and his family after they met in South Africa. They had kept in touch, and she regularly shared pictures of her work as a tour guide across the continent.

"Raz, please bring Rory up to speed. What do we know so far?" Ranger Adia asked.

"Snuggles' paw prints led us to the far west corner of the park. Then, suddenly, at the edge of the car park, the trail goes cold. No more paw prints."

"Our deduction is he has been... stolen."

"What?... are you sure?" Rory asked.

"Yes, we are." Chidinma said, locking eyes with Rory. "However, there is something else you should know..."

PLANS AND PIGEONS

Rory sat down at the table as Chidinma placed several photos in front of him.

"Snuggles is the latest in a series of cute, cuddly canines to go missing from the park. We noticed the trend a few weeks ago, not just in South London but across the city. After some great detective work by Raz and Elon, we uncovered the culprits. It appears a rogue crew of feisty foxes have been freely roaming the fields picking up the precious pups."

"Where have they been taken?" Rory asked.

Chiku rolled out a map and set of building blueprints and pointed to the marked location.

"Here. An old disused factory. The foxes have also had a lot of deliveries the past few days, so it seems our canine friends are well fed." Chiku gestured to a picture showing a dog food truck arriving at the factory.

"It's under the arches near Waterloo station in central London. Fortunately, we are in close contact with our pigeon team, who are keeping a close look out." Chiku picked up a remote control and switched on the large flatscreen TV behind Rory. Immediately multiple video feeds were on the screen, which appeared to show various entrances and exits to the factory. "Most people see pigeons as an unhelpful element of city life. However, if they knew how many crucial rescue missions they have been involved with, I think opinions would change." Chiku held down the button on the stand-up microphone in front of him. "Penelope, it's Chiku. What is the latest situation on the ground?"

A pigeon's head lent into the video camera, far too close to focus, and a whispered voice murmured. "Penelope, we can't hear you. Is everything OK?"

"We have a situation CCHQ, the gang is preparing to move. We saw them at the station sneakily stealing a map and guidebook for the City of Oxford," Penelope reported.

"That's fortunate. My class at school are due to be travelling to Oxford tomorrow to visit the Roger Bannister Running Track," Rory announced.

"Excellent! We can join up with you under the cover of darkness via a portal. I've always wanted to go visit such a famous city and a site of running greatness," Chiku said.

"Rory, take this earpiece so we can communicate and go back home. Tomorrow we are going to rescue Snuggles and stop the fox gang once and for all!" Chidinma said.

Rory nodded, placed the earpiece in his pocket, and opened the door back to the tunnel. "See you there, team." The door closed, and he went on his way back home with an extra spring in his step and determined to make his first mission a success.

OXFORD BOUND

Unsurprisingly, Rory didn't sleep much that night. Instead, he caught some extra rest on the train journey from London to Oxford, clinging tightly to his rucksack, which held his precious Cheetah Club race jersey.

On arrival at the famous running track, his earpiece beeped. Fortunately, Rory's mousey tousled hair covered his ears and the earpiece, keeping it hidden from his classmates and teachers.

"Rory, this is CCHQ, over."

"Roger that CCHQ, over."

"Er... Rory, are you talking to yourself?" a teacher asked, confusion etched across his face.

"Ah, er yes, just practising some lines from the school summer play," Rory said as he walked away to a quieter place.

"Rory, what is your status? The fox gang are on the move and travelling up the motorway having hitched a ride with the kidnapped dogs in the back of a horsebox! Adia is following on a tour bus," Chiku said.

"I'm outside the racetrack; keep me posted," Rory said.

After the conversation ended, Rory reflected on the thought of a horsebox full of foxes and dogs. Imagine the confusion on the driver's face if he checks inside! He chuckled to himself before his attention was taken by the plaque in front of him. It read, *"Here at the Iffley Road Track, the first sub-four-minute mile was run on 6th May 1954 by ROGER BANNISTER."* Chills ran through Rory's body as he imagined what had occurred sixty-seven years earlier on the ground where he was standing. It was a truly momentous achievement that changed the course of distance running and the mindset of human potential forever! Rory was in awe, and his mind pictured that day many years ago, as he dreamed of running as fast himself in the future. It made him more excited than ever to put on his running shoes on this crisp, sunny September day in the heart of England.

In fact, Rory was so distracted he didn't see Steady Eddie sneaking up behind him. "Boo!" Eddie shouted as he bumped into Rory, startling him and knocking his earpiece out of his ear into his bag.

"Oi!" Rory responded, gathering himself.

"Sorry, just passing on the message from the teachers. It's time to get changed, mate!" Eddie said.

"OK, race you there!" Rory replied. The two shot off to catch up with the group on the way to the changing rooms.

Shortly afterwards, Rory stepped onto the rubber track alongside his friend, Stella. No words were spoken as they took in the moment. After a few laps, the class were taken on a historical tour.

"Did you know Sir Roger practised medicine for sixty years, writing over eighty papers on neurology, the study of the brain. He is said to have considered his contribution to medicine his greatest achievement ahead of his running breakthrough."

Rory heard a beeping from his bag. *Oh no, the earpiece*, he thought. Telling the group he needed to go to the bathroom, he walked away from the group and rummaged in his bag for the device. Frantically, he placed it in his ear.

"CCHQ, Rory here, sorry I was distracted. What is going on?"

"Rory, we have no time to waste. The fox gang is nearby, the driver has turned off the motorway, and we believe he is headed for the service station to stop to refuel. The service station is a mile from your location. Can you get there quickly and stop their progress while we catch up?"

"Er... I will do my best, but I'll need some help."

Rory sneaked back towards the group and beckoned Stella over to him. "Psst, Stella..." he whispered. Eventually, she saw him and slowly backed away from her classmates.

"What is it, Rory?" Stella asked.

Rory took a step back and stood in front of Stella with his arms wide and palms open. "I need your help on a rescue mission with my running club who are nearby. I can't do it alone, and I'm sure you have lots of questions; however, it's a long story, and there is little time, so I'll explain along the way. Will you come with me?"

Stella agreed.

SECRETS AND SUPPORT

As they jogged towards the service station, Rory explained, as best he could, about his trip to Africa and the talking animals he'd met. He told her about the cheetahs and their underground city and how he was now part of their running club. Stella stayed silent as she took it all in.

"...and now Snuggles needs our help, and the gang who have taken him are at the service station. We need to stall them while the club travels to meet us through the Sir Roger Bannister running track portal," Rory said.

"Wait, hang on a minute," Stella interjected. "You expect me to believe these safari animals can walk, talk, travel through the world instantaneously, and are a secret animal rescue crew who fit in a bit of

45

running from time to time?" she said with disbelief in her voice.

"Well, er, yes..." Rory replied, realising how crazy his story sounded.

"If we had more time, I could explain, but we need to stop the fox gang. Please trust me. I need your help."

Stella paused in thought and took in a deep breath. "OK, but I'm only doing this to save the dog, not because I believe you."

Not for the first time, Rory's sincerity and the desire to help others had convinced his friend.

Rory thanked Stella. Now time was running out before the horsebox would be back on the road.

Horse Box Happenings

Rory glanced from left to right. "OK, you distract the driver. He's gone to the service station to pay for the fuel. I will let out the air from the horsebox tyres to stall their progress and investigate the contents."

It sounded like a plan, so Stella readied herself to enter the service station shop, get in front of the driver in the queue and delay him by taking an unbelievably long time buying a bottle of water.

The two avid runners set off in separate directions. Stella darted towards the service station shop whilst Rory sneaked round the back to the horse cart. Rory could see the checkout in the shop from his position, which helped him keep a close eye on Stella's progress. Fortunately, it looked like the driver was browsing for snacks, and there was a big queue to the checkout, so he had a few minutes at least, no time to lose!

As Rory arrived at the horsebox, he could hear snoring from inside. Stepping up on the right rear wheel, he pulled himself up to look through the small window. Scanning the interior, Rory saw four dogs and five foxes separated by a partition. The animals were sleeping, and the dogs looked relaxed. To his surprise, they were stretched out on luxurious pillows and blankets with plenty of food and doggy treats present alongside ornate water bowls. He focused in, and in the far corner could see Snuggles, who was living up to his name, and snuggling between two prize pooches.

Rory needed to attract Snuggles' attention. Swiftly moving around to the left tyre, Rory could get just above Snuggles' head. He tapped gently, but no response, "Snuggles, psst," he whispered, but nothing happened. Rory stepped back, considering his options. Aha! I need a poking device, he thought. After finding a long twig, he managed to lever it into position through the small opening beneath the door of the horsebox and prod Snuggles. Two more prods and Snuggles jolted up onto his feet. Suddenly it occurred to Rory, he hadn't considered how he would communicate with the dog. He had just assumed he'd be able to talk! Would Snuggles understand him?

Fortunately, Mrs Partridge had given Rory some of Snuggles' favourite treats and a picture of her with the dog from her handbag. He waved them both at the startled dog, he started wagging his tail. Then, having realised the back door was secured only by a latch, Rory managed to open it and enter.

Snuggles immediately ran to Rory, looked at the picture, then happily munched on the snacks.

"This does not look like a kidnapping," Rory murmured to himself.

"Kidnapping? What kidnapping? Whose been kidnapped?" Snuggles barked.

Rory had his answer. Either all animals could now talk, or he had found a unique ability to hear them. There was no time to figure this out right now. He would just have to accept it.

"Ssshhh!" whispered Rory, putting his finger to his lips.

"Er, hello, Snuggles, you ... you have been kidnapped from your owner Mrs Partridge."

"Ha don't be silly, nothing could be further from the truth – we are helping our fox friends," Snuggles replied.

"What? How? Why are you in a horsebox bound for Oxford?"

"Let me explain..."

SNUGGLES' STORY

"Come, sit next to me. They won't wake," Snuggles said, reassuring Rory as he looked at the three other canines in the horsebox snoozing on the luxuriously soft furnishings. He went and joined Snuggles on his silk, feather-filled cushion with golden tassels as the poodle started his story.

"I was in the park minding my own business when from behind the Cypress Oak in the wooded area on the north side of the park, a noise attracted my attention. On approaching, I was greeted by a fox. He was not looking in the best of shape and appeared upset. In conversation, it became apparent that he and his fellow foxes felt threatened by humans in the city. Dogs had managed to befriend their human masters and be welcomed into their homes. The fox said this was hugely desirable for the fox community and asked, given my privileged status with Mrs Partridge, living in her grand house, which the foxes wished to emulate, would I come meet with Frederick, the fox leader. He wanted me to help them learn the skills necessary to improve their relations with the human population," Snuggles explained.

"OK, makes sense, sort of. So why did you leave London, and why are you in a horsebox on your way to Oxford?" Rory asked.

"Ah, well, you see, having trained the foxes in the ways of a dog, and despite acquiring a high degree of dog-like tendencies through their discipline and hard work, the humans still rejected their approaches. It was clear the foxes were feared by the humans, and I concluded they had to find a way to look more like dogs, not just act like them. I remembered my neighbours' dog, Sheeba, who uncannily resembled a fox. She is a Shiba Inu, and her ancestors resided in Japan. So, we are travelling to Oxford Airport to commandeer a plane and fly to Japan to help the fox population learn from and integrate into the Shiba Inu community. After their training, the foxes will return home and look to get adopted by humans across the world who believe them to be Shiba Inu dogs. Once they have proven themselves to be good pets, they will reveal themselves to their hosts as foxes. The goal is to show foxes in a new light, capable of living alongside humans and improving human and fox relations for generations to come!" Snuggles finished talking with a flourish; the excitement in his voice pulled him onto his feet in anticipation.

"Er, wow, that is a commendable goal, Snuggles. Sorry to burst your bubble, but... firstly, planes from Oxford Airport don't travel to Japan. I would also be surprised if a dog or fox could fly the plane if you commandeer it. However, I do have another idea on how we can get there," Rory said.

"Excellent... and you said we... Are you going to help us? I mean, help the foxes get the acceptance and equality they desire and deserve from humans?" Snuggles said, looking sincerely at Rory.

"Yes, this is a mission for The Cheetah Cub Running Club!" declared Rory.

TRACK TROUBLE

Rory arrived back at the agreed meeting spot, finding Stella already there. "Er... why are the truck and horsebox driving off, Rory?" Stella asked.

"Change of plan. Let's get back to the running track. I'll explain on the way," Rory replied.

Stella sighed and rolled her eyes as she got up and jogged to catch up with Rory, who had already set off.

On the way back, Rory told Stella of his conversation with Snuggles. Stella was still bemused and not convinced of the idea of talking animals.

"So, you see, Stella, I've told Snuggles to request the foxes reroute to the running track instead of the airport. We can meet up with the Cheetah Club there. As Japan has just held the Olympic Games, and the Cheetah Club can portal to and from any running track in the world, this will help the foxes get to Japan," Rory said.

Stella frowned.

"OK, however, have you considered if this is a good idea, Rory? The foxes are wild animals and not domesticated. Could it not be dangerous to have foxes inside houses with young children? And have you asked the Cheetah Club if they are willing to give permission to use the portal to go to Japan?"

"Ah, they'll be fine – I'm a member now, so I'm not sure I technically need permission," Rory said.

The two runners arrived back at the running track just as the truck and horse cart pulled in.

Moments later, Rory's earpiece pinged, and he answered.

"Rory, we are just arriving at the portal near the entrance of the running track. Where are you, and what is your status? Over," Chiku said.

"Roger that, HQ, I'm at the running track and have a lot to update you on. The foxes haven't kidnapped Snuggles, they just want to be more like dogs, and he is helping them domesticate. Over."

"Don't be so sure, Rory. The foxes may have ulterior motives. Be wary of them, and don't take everything at face value. We will be arriving in five minutes."

Just then, Snuggles exited the horsebox alongside a tall, slender fox. They walked over to Rory, who was standing next to Stella.

"Rory, let me introduce you to Frederick Fox, the London Fox Community leader," Snuggles said.

"Pleasure to meet you, Mr Fox. This is my friend, Stella," Rory replied.

"The pleasure is all mine, Rory. Oh, and please call me Frederick. I'm not for formality," he said with some reverence.

Stella's mouth dropped open. So, it was true, the animals could talk!

"Of course, er, Frederick. I understand you want to learn from the dog community about being 'man's best friend' so you and your fellow foxes can similarly get invited to live alongside humans in their homes. Do I have that right?" Rory asked.

"Yes," Frederick replied.

"It seems strange as foxes are not an endangered species. I understand some fox species such as the Hoary Fox and Sierra Nevada Red Fox are on the decline, but there are hundreds of thousands of foxes in the

UK. So why do you want to give up being wild and free?" Rory asked.

"Indeed, that is our desire, young Rory. Our life is not one of joy, particularly in London. We are ridiculed, feared, attacked and evicted from the very land we have lived on for hundreds of years. The biggest threat to our lives is humans. So infiltrating, sorry, improving our relations with humans can only help the survival of my kind," Frederick replied.

"Are you sure you were not kidnapping the dogs, Mr Fox?" Stella asked Frederick, staring at him.

"No, not at all. In fact, we have made our dog friends our VIP guests. Just ask Mr Snuggles here," Frederick said, shifting his eyes to the dog by his side.

"Yes, that is right, nothing but the best has been provided to us during our time with the foxes," Snuggles replied.

"Excuse us for a moment," Rory said, gesturing to Stella to follow him a few steps away from the fox and dog.

"Stella, why are you being rude to Frederick? He needs our help."

"I'm not so sure, Rory. He seems dodgy to me. It's rather convenient. I suggest we speak to the other dogs in the fox's company before we consider helping them," Stella said.

Rory took a moment to think. He felt he was a good judge of character; however, Stella had a point.

"Hmm, well, we don't have much time. Let's see what the Cheetah Club says when they get here."

61

They heard rustling in the trees, and Chiku, Raz and Elon walked out, joined by Ranger Adia. "Hello, team. So pleased to see you here. We have a lot to update you on," Rory said to the new arrivals.

"Let me introduce you to Stella and..." Rory stopped abruptly as he realised Frederick and Snuggles were nowhere to be seen. "Where did they go?"

"Rory!" Elon said breathlessly. "We've been trying to reach you on your earpiece to warn you!"

Rory felt for his ear and realised the earpiece wasn't there and must have fallen out.

"Warn me about what?" Rory asked.

"We uncovered information that Frederick Fox is a rogue fox agent and has been working on an evil plan to replace cats and dogs with foxes as human's favourite pets. The dogs and cats will be evicted from their human homes with nowhere to live. The foxes will use their new position of power as the head of the domesticated animal kingdom to rule over gardens and parks of cities around the world to the detriment of all other animals. He cannot be trusted!" Raz said.

Rory's mind raced; his mouth dropped. "Oh no! Snuggles thinks he is being kind by helping the foxes, and I told him about the portal!"

The group all turned around in unison to face the trees where the portal was hidden, just in time to see Snuggles and Frederick entering…

JAPAN-BOUND!

The group ran towards the trees. "Stop, Rory, it's not safe!" Raz called out as Rory had rapidly made his way to the tree line.

Rory came to an abrupt halt. "Let's go. We haven't got a lot of time!"

"Raz is right, Rory; the portal will become unstable if there are too many travellers at the same time. Particularly if going to different destinations," Chiku said.

"But I know where they're heading," Rory replied.

"Where?" Chiku asked.

"They're going to Japan."

Elon, Raz and Chiku looked at each other, deciphering the information.

Rory interrupted, "They want to infiltrate the Shiba Inu dog community, so

64

humans unsuspectingly adopt them into their homes."

"OK, well, let's go then. We have only set up one portal so far in Japan, and that is at the Japan National Stadium. Follow me!" Chiku said.

"Hang on!" shouted Stella. "Rory, you expect me to get into a strange space and time tunnel with a group of talking animals without any explanation. This is crazy!"

"I understand how strange this seems. However, has anything I said so far turned out not to be true?" Rory asked.

"Er ... no," replied Stella.

"And when are you going to get the chance to see, or maybe race at the Japan National Stadium?" Rory asked.

"OK, you convinced me. I'm as ready as I'll ever be."

Rory and Stella followed Chiku, Elon, Raz and Adia down the tunnel and came to the familiar wooden door Rory had become so accustomed to.

"Chiku, how do we get to Japan and not back to the secret city?" Rory asked.

"I've spoken to HQ. They put the correct coordinates in, so we exit at the correct destination when we open the door. Let's see if it worked," Chiku said with a wry smile.

Raz opened the door. The sun shone into the Cheetah Club members' eyes. They stepped out into the dazzling daylight. Immediately before them was the imposing, impressive structure known as the Japan National Stadium. Just weeks before, it had seen some of the most amazing feats of human performance and now, they were standing in its shadow. Rory and Stella were itching to get inside and get on the track.

"Right, let's focus, team. We must find Frederick and Snuggles and warn the Shiba Inu community before it's too late," Chiku said.

"I know where we need to go, follow me," she continued. The group gathered and followed their leader into the streets ahead.

TIME TICKING IN TOKYO

The Cheetah Cub Running Club made their way south through the vibrant, thriving, techno-colour metropolis to Tokyo's most famous dog meeting spot – the Hachiko Memorial Statue at Shibuya station. "Hachiko, an Akita dog, was considered the most loyal dog of all. He has his own statue in his honour at the corner of the station where he waited for his owner each day. He continued to do so for over nine years after his owner's death," Chiku said.

"Wow, that is some level of commitment. I struggle to wait nine minutes when cooking my dinner!" Elon joked.

On arrival, Chiku ran towards the statue. On the left side was an older Shiba Inu, pacing back and forth.

"You must be Satoshi."

"Yes, I am. You must be Chiku. Chidinma said you had some important information for me to protect my community?" Satoshi said.

Satoshi was the leader of the Shiba Inu population in Tokyo.

"There is a feisty fox who has found his way from England who goes by the name of Frederick. He is travelling with a poodle named Snuggles and wants to infiltrate the Shiba Inu community with foxes to replace dogs and cats as the favourite pets of humans. If they succeed, not only will it mean less humans to adopt your fellow canines, but it will also lead to calamity within the homes. We, The Cheetah Cub Running Club, are a global animal rescue crew. We are here to put a stop to this but do not know where they may be. Where is the most likely place they will have gone to find Shiba Inu up for adoption?" Chiku asked.

"The dog cafés. We have several them around the city, mainly with Mame Shiba, the smaller of the breed. Whilst they are not commonly up for adoption, I'm sure the owners could be convinced," Satoshi replied.

"OK great, where are the cafés?" Raz asked.

"Well, you see, that's your problem, there are six main cafés, all over the great city of Tokyo," Satoshi said.

Chiku looked at the map. "Let's split up. There are six of us and six cafés. Here's a new earpiece for each of us. We must keep in touch and confirm as soon as you encounter either Frederick or Snuggles."

Rory, Stella, Adia, Elon and Raz nodded.

Satoshi pulled out a map and showed each team member the café they were to go to.

"Best of luck, comrades," Rory said.

It was time to roll.

FIND THAT FOX!

Elon was the first to arrive at his designated dog café, a small shop in the Akihabara district in Tokyo. Despite the fact he couldn't enter through the tiny doorway, it took no time at all to determine that Frederick and Snuggles were not present after peering through the glass and using his trunk to poke in each of the corners.

Raz, Chiku, Adia and Rory had similar results at their locations, no sightings of the fox or dog either in the flesh or by the café owners in recent hours.

On the other hand, Stella had picked up a trail immediately on arrival at Harajuku Mama Shiba café.

"Hello, have you had a fox or poodle come visit today?" Stella asked.

The owner responded in Japanese, tapping his ear and shaking his head, unable to understand Stella's English.

Stella took the mugshot of Frederick that Chiku had given each member of the team and showed it to the owner.

Suddenly, the owner's demeanour changed. His smile dropped, and he looked from side to side before vigorously pointing into the back, nervously. Stella put the required entry fee in coins on the counter and moved past the owner, following the direction he was pointing.

Stella pressed the button on the side of her earpiece. "Team, I have a feeling Frederick has been to my location. If I confirm a sighting, I will let you know immediately. Stay on this channel, over."

Each team member acknowledged.

"Rory, you're the closest to Stella's location. If you're confident our targets are not at your café, go provide support," Chiku said.

"Roger that," Rory replied.

On entering the café, Stella was met with a wave of beautiful, bouncy, bubbly Mame Shiba dogs. All were eager to see a new arrival and welcome her in. She respectfully accepted their affections as she picked each one of them up to check they were not, in fact, a fox!

Over in the far corner, Stella spotted a bushy tail attached to the final inhabitant, slowly shifting towards the doorway. Swiftly speeding with certainty, Stella managed to cut off the escapee. She paused momentarily in shock. It was Frederick! "Not so fast, Frederick!" Stella shouted.

Frederick immediately darted back into the pack of dogs. Stella could not see him in the swarm. Where did he go? Stella foraged frantically through the throng, trying to find the fox.

At this point, Rory arrived.

"Block the door!" shouted Stella.

It was too late. At least half the pack of dogs had migrated out of the room after the commotion started. Frederick was gone.

FRANTIC CHASE

"I saw him. He's masquerading as a dog. Where could he have gone?" Stella wondered.

Rory paused for a second. Just then, a car's engine fired up right outside the café and sped off. Screams were heard as it careered through the street, nearly hitting innocent bystanders and almost smashing into at least two parked vehicles. Rory and Stella ran to the window to see where it was headed. Rory got on his radio earpiece.

"HQ, can you track a green Mazda heading due north from our location. Over."

"Roger that. We have a lock on a green Mazda. The registered owner is the head of the Japanese animal adoption agency! They appear to be heading directly for the national stadium," Chidinma replied.

"THE PORTAL!" Rory and Stella said in unison, looking at each other in exasperation. They flew out the door and sprinted after the car.

Raz, Elon, Adia and Chiku had heard the communication and were on their way back to the stadium. Raz and Chiku were in the back of a delivery van provided by Satoshi and driven by Ranger Adia. Elon was well on his way back to the stadium on foot. They would most likely get to the stadium before Rory and Stella – quite possibly before the getaway vehicle.

"Elon, go directly to the portal and block the entrance. Raz, you and I will target the vehicle. We'll look to contain it and speak to the inhabitants," Chiku said through her earpiece.

Back on the streets of Tokyo, the car swung from side to side as it manoeuvred towards the stadium, dangerously navigating its way, disregarding the traffic lights and stop signs. The traffic was unforgiving, stalling the frustrated fox and his comrade. Rory and Stella were catching up and could see the situation unfolding inside. It appeared a man had his hands tied and was sitting in the rear and... Frederick was steering, using a metal pole to press the pedals. Snuggles looked worried.

"Team, we have managed to infiltrate the speaker system inside the target vehicle. We can listen in to the conversation and will play through your earpieces via a translation system," Chidinma informed the group.

"Roger that," replied Chiku.

Immediately, a grainy conversation could be heard.

"You cannot do this. This is insane! How can you expect me to find a thousand homes for foxes pretending to be Shiba Inu dogs!" It was the head of the animal adoption agency!

"Oh, you will do it, sir. Or we will open up the portal to one million foxes who will come to Tokyo!" Frederick threatened menacingly.

"It's your choice; one thousand foxes or one million foxes. We will channel the foxes from the portal into the stadium, disguise them as Shiba Inu dogs, and you will declare on national television that you are donating the prized dogs to 1,000 homes around the city. Do you understand?" Frederick said.

The man nodded in defeat. He did not believe he had any other option.

"Why are you doing this, Frederick? I thought you wanted to live in harmony with humans and dogs?" Snuggles said, concerned.

"Stop being so slow to realise, dog.

Dogs do not mean anything to me, nor do humans. I am focused not just on the survival of the fox community but the domination over all city-living animals for generations. By infiltrating the human's homes, we will be in a position of great power and will truly rule over you and the dog community forever!" Frederick laughed at Snuggles with a crazy look in his eyes.

"Team, we must stop the announcement from happening, and we have to stop the foxes entering via the portal. Elon, what is your position? Over," Chiku asked.

"I am just arriving now. Over," Elon replied.

"OK, enter the tunnel of the portal and stop any unexpected visitors coming through. Let the team know if you encounter any trouble. Over," Chiku said.

"Raz, Adia and I are almost at the stadium. We'll try to dismantle the communication and networking equipment. Rory, Stella, what's your status?" Chiku continued.

"We... have... the... vehicle... in our sights." Rory gasped as he sprinted.

"Good, try to delay the vehicle in any way you can."

"Roger."

Rory and Stella pulled up alongside the car transporting the kidnappers and their hostage at the next junction. Snuggles had no way through so had to wait for the traffic to clear. Stella knocked on the window. Both Frederick and Snuggles froze.

"Stop the car!" Stella shouted.

"No way!" The crazed fox shouted at Stella.

Frederick grimaced, gesturing to Snuggles to get moving.

The car shot forward into a gap between two buses, the stadium could be seen ahead.

HISSSSSS

Just as the car moved, it veered off to the slide and rolled to a stop. Rory had managed to deflate a tyre while Stella had distracted the getaway drivers.

ARGH!

"You can't stop us! Sir, get ready. We are going to stream your announcement live from your website," Frederick said, pulling out the man's phone from his coat."

What were The Cheetah Cub Running Club to do now?

THE ANNOUNCEMENT

Frederick held the phone up to the mayor's face, careful not to show his restrained arms. Rory and Stella urgently tried to unlock the door.

The stream went live.

"Er, I have a special announcement to make..." the man started... "Today, we are looking for a thousand caring households to come to the national stadium for a great cause ..." he continued.

Suddenly, Stella appeared next to the man, having navigated her way in from the unlocked trunk – she whispered something in his ear. He smiled...

"… We are going to hold a fun run to celebrate the anniversary of the Hachiko statue being unveiled. All owners and their dogs are welcome ... see you at 3 p.m.!" he said in Japanese.

She grabbed the phone and threw it out the window for Rory, who caught it!

"No! You can't do that!" Frederick screamed.

"I warned you. We will now flood the town with foxes!" He grabbed his walkie-talkie and spoke.

"To all fox group leaders around the world, execute Operation Flood!" Frederick sneered and then laughed menacingly.

Nothing happened.

Another minute passed...nothing. Frederick looked confused.

He spoke again into his walkie-talkie. "Er... guys... is anyone there?" By now, the operation should have been in motion and the first fox gangs should be arriving in town via the portal.

"Ahem, this is Francesca Fox from the International Fox Foundation. Operation Flood has been aborted."

"What?! That's not possible. I am the highest-ranking fox official. I demand you execute the plan," Frederick ordered.

"You are no longer the highest-ranking, Frederick. While you were in Tokyo, The Cheetah Cub Running Club HQ got in touch with us via the Oxford fox group, who met Elon at the portal entrance in Tokyo. They shared with us your sneaky plan and an alternative of how we could live in harmony with our humans by understanding each other and respecting each other's needs and space. We have also joined the local Cheetah Cub Running Club community run in the evenings whilst the humans are sleeping.

There is no need to infiltrate the dog community. We need to be true to ourselves rather than trying to be something we are not," Francesca continued.

Frederick shook his head, "No, no, no! We need to take our rightful place in ruling over the other urban animals."

"I'm sorry, Frederick. It is over," Francesca said. The Cheetah Cub Running Club will escort you back to the UK, where you will be informed of your new duties serving the community better."

Rory untied the head of the animal adoption agency, who took over control of his vehicle. "To the stadium, please," he said.

STADIUM DELIGHT

By now, the group were all back together outside the stadium.

"Frederick, Francesca is right. Foxes can live in harmony with other communities. We have proven it ourselves," Chiku said, as Elon, Raz, Rory, Adia, and Stella nodded and smiled in agreement.

"Go and see for yourself inside the stadium."

Frederick walked up the stairs in the stand. He could hear a joyous chorus of chatter, laughter, and barking. He breathed deeply as he took in the beautiful sight before him. The remainder of the group joined him in silence.

Families, dogs, enjoyment, and exercise. The head of the animal adoption agency took the stage in the centre of the field inside the track.

"Ladies and gentlemen, boys, girls, dogs and all our fellow friends of any kind. I am so pleased we have come together to celebrate the life of Hachiko. He was loyal and knew the importance of supporting his loved one as we support one another. I would like to take this opportunity to request that we support and live in harmony with all animals and look after the environment in our great city, being an example around the world for positive change. Enjoy your run!" He smiled up at the stand, acknowledging the crew.

Stella tapped Frederick on the shoulder and gestured for him to join her down on the track.

"Go on, try it out. You may just enjoy it," Chiku said.

Frederick shrugged his shoulders and followed Stella. Rory was not going to miss the chance to run in such an iconic stadium.

If Frederick was in awe of the view from the stand, being down in the arena, centre stage, was an entirely different level of experience: the smell of rubber, the bounce underfoot, the atmosphere of anticipation. Frederick's worry that a fox would not be accepted or would be ridiculed, pointed at, even rejected, proved unfounded. He relaxed, pushed his shoulders back and started to trot. There was joy in the air and a buzz of excitement. So many champions had trod these steps, broken records. History had been made right here in this spot.

Rory and Stella jogged a step behind, not wanting to dilute the moment for the fox ahead of them. They shared a satisfied smile between them; this would be a memory etched in their mind forever.

"OK, I get it, we can live in harmony by accepting each other for who we are and being true to ourselves. Foxes are foxes, not dogs, and humans are humans," Frederick said.

Stella smiled. "That's humble of you, Frederick. However, I think humans also need to be more aware of the impact we have on our natural habitat and that of the animals who also call Planet Earth home."

"I'm sorry for the trouble I caused. Is there anything I can do to help rectify my actions?"

"We continue to try and educate by being role models for others in living healthy and respectful lives side by side with the animal community. I suggest that going forward, you live your life doing the same, helping others less fortunate," Rory replied.

Frederick nodded. "I will do so."

Stella and Rory acknowledged Frederick's sincerity and concession, and they agreed on a plan on how they could support each other when they got back to the United Kingdom. But that could wait until they had raced!

SNUGGLES RETURNED

As the day drew to a close, Rory and Stella walked either side of Snuggles as they exited the portal in Dulwich Park, back in London.

"I'm so sorry for the trouble I've caused. How could I be so naïve?" Snuggles said.

Rory ruffled Snuggle's fur. "Don't you worry, my friend, everyone makes mistakes. I ignored all the signs as well. We just need to ensure we learn from them."

"If it wasn't for you, we would not have caught Frederick and stopped his plan, so things have worked out for the best," Stella added.

Just then, Mrs Partridge could be seen in the distance, walking briskly towards them with her arms open wide.

"OK, back to barking for me now." Snuggles sighed. "However, I am so grateful to have a home and loving owner."

Mrs Partridge arrived and embraced her prized poodle. "Snuggles! My sweet Snuggles, where have you been?"

"Oh, he was just stuck down a fox hole Mrs Partridge. Took a while to get him out but he's safe and sound now." Rory replied, thinking quickly on his feet.

"Thank you so much."

"Our pleasure."

Mrs Partridge walked off, tugging gently at the newly attached lead on Snuggles' collar. Snuggles looked behind as he was pulled along with an expression of resignation and relaxation.

Rory and Stella high fived and laughed. A job well done.

"Oh, by the way, Stella, Chiku and Chidinma wanted me to give you this," Rory said, giving her an envelope. She opened it. Putting her hand to her mouth, she gasped.

"It's an invitation to the secret city... to receive my Cheetah Cub Running Club jersey!" Stella said with delight.

"I couldn't think of anyone more deserving. Now come on, let's race," Rory replied.

"Don't we need to get back to Oxford?" Stella asked.

"Ah, yes. We'll race back to the portal. Bet you can't catch me," he shouted as he shot off round the bridleway.

Stella laughed, looked around and took in the tranquil surroundings in her hometown. She had never been so happy and fulfilled. What would the future hold? She didn't know for sure but knew she wanted to make a difference and being a member of The Cheetah Cub Running Club would give her the chance to do that. So many adventures lay ahead but now, it was time to focus.

"Rory, you've got no chance," Stella said as she launched into a sprint and ran off in search of Rory as the sun settled on the South London park on this special September evening.

The End

PLEASE WRITE A REVIEW

Authors love hearing from their readers!

Please let Philip Laslett know what you thought about *The Cheetah Cub Running Club* by leaving a review on **cheetahcubrunning.club/books**

Philip will always reply to you ☺

If under 13, please ask a grown-up to help you

And if they can help you copy your review to Amazon or your other preferred online bookstore it will help more parents and children find *The Cheetah Cub Running Club.*

THANK YOU FROM RORY & STELLA!

JOIN OUR NEWLETTER!

Sneak peaks, news and updates of future releases and request advanced reader copies of upcoming books.

Get an **exclusive FREE Cheetah Cub Running Club values poster**!

Scan For Your Free Poster:
If under 13, please ask a grown-up to help you

ABOUT THE AUTHOR

Runnerwhowrites.com

Philip Laslett is a children's author and keen runner based in London, England. His books aim to entertain and encourage children to build self-confidence through the enjoyment of exercise and expressing their creativity. He has written four books. Three of which are available as paperbacks in the Cheetah Cub Running Club Series.

facebook.com/philiplaslettauthor

tiktok.com/@philiplaslettauthor

twitter.com/philiplaslett

Instagram.com/philiplaslettauthor

youtube.com/philiplaslettauthor

ACKNOWLEDGEMENTS

On 27th May 2017, I stood at the start line of Dulwich Parkrun for the first time. Nervous, and apprehensive. Little did I know it would be the kindle that lit my fire and started me on a journey to rediscover my love of running. Running has developed into a key part of my life over the past four years. In particular, I would like to thank the amazing volunteers and runners of Parkrun and my neighbour, Jeremy, who encouraged me to give it a go (and gave me a lift) back on that late summer morning.

No matter your age or fitness level, Parkrun is so welcoming and I recommend checking it out and discovering for yourself at www.parkrun.org.uk

Thanks go once again to my editor, Amanda and cover design illustrator Agnes, who are so good at what they do. I am also grateful, and thankful once again to my family who support me and inspire me in my writing and running on a daily basis.

Get your FREE copy of The Cheetah Cub Running Club PREQUEL: Where It All Began

It is 1921 and a cheetah coalition is struggling. Lack of food and water, threats from Hyenas at every corner. Reliant on Chaka, a young adolescent cheetah, to provide for them. The odds are against them.

How are they going to survive? What can they do to ensure their future?

Chad, a senior cheetah, has an idea...

Scan to get your FREE book:

OTHER BOOKS BY PHILIP LASLETT

The Cheetah Cub Running Club (Book 1)

In Africa, on a conservation trip with his father, ten-year-old 'Rapid' Rory discovers a secret city ran by a group of animals whose habitat is under threat. Rory must work with animals, known collectively as the Cheetah Cub Running Club, to protect the city from being taken over by their arch enemies the Heavenly Hyenas.

Will they survive? Can Rory and the Cheetah Cub Running Club beat the Hyenas in a race for the keys to the city?

The Cheetah Cub Running Club (Book 3): An American Adventure

Chiku, The Cheetah Club leader is imprisoned! Thousands of miles from home, without any means of communication. Chiku's captor, a circus master with a bitter past, is determined to get rich, and doesn't care what damage he does in the process. He's taken many animals against their will, and they need help and fast!

Can The Cheetah Club Running Club rescue the vulnerable circus animals before they are forced to perform? Will they be able to protect their compromised network and community?

The teams search takes them across the United States, culminating in Boston, where they must draw on the past to save the future.

Order online, at your local bookshop or find out more at cheetahcubrunning.club/books

Made in the USA
Monee, IL
10 December 2022